Useful Tails

Ted O'Hare

Bethany, Missouri

Photo Credits:
Cover © Michelle Allen; Title Page © Photodisc; Page 4 © Martin Plsek; Pages 5, 6, 7, 9, 15, 22 © Photodisc;
Page 10 © Phaedra Wilkinson; Page 11 © Fernando; Page 12 © John Billingslea Jr.; Page 13 ©
Steve McSweeny; Page 14 © Goran Cakmazovic; Page 16 © Edzard de Ranitz; Page 17 © Jason Wassing;
Page 18 © Tony Campbell; Page 19 © Tom Delme; Page 21 © Nico Smit

Cataloging-in-Publication Data

O'Hare, Ted, 1961-
    Useful tails / Ted O'Hare. — 1st ed.
    p. cm. — (Animal features)

    Includes bibliographical references and index.
    Summary: Text and photographs showcase the
tails of various animals, including how these extremities
are used and why they are important.
    ISBN-13: 978-1-4242-1406-8 (lib. bdg. : alk. paper)
    ISBN-10: 1-4242-1406-8 (lib. bdg. : alk. paper)
    ISBN-13: 978-1-4242-1496-9 (pbk. : alk. paper)
    ISBN-10: 1-4242-1496-3 (pbk. : alk. paper)

    1. Tail—Juvenile literature. [1. Tail. 2. Animals.]
I. O'Hare, Ted, 1961- II. Title. III. Series.
    QL950.6.O43 2007
    591.4—dc22

First edition
© 2007 Fitzgerald Books
802 N. 41st Street, P.O. Box 505
Bethany, MO 64424, U.S.A.
Printed in China
Library of Congress Control Number: 2006911286

Table of Contents

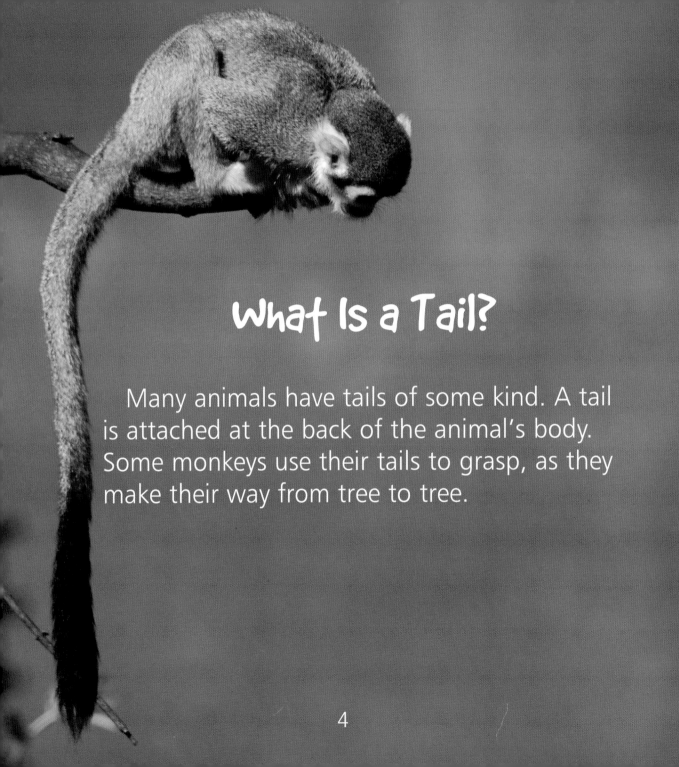

What Is a Tail?

Many animals have tails of some kind. A tail is attached at the back of the animal's body. Some monkeys use their tails to grasp, as they make their way from tree to tree.

5

Tails come in many shapes and sizes. They may be covered with fur or they may be plain.

Tails may be short or long. They may even be curly.

Different Kinds of Tails

A beaver's tail is broad and flat. It supports the beaver while it does its work.

9

When a dog wags its tail, it means that the dog is happy.

But when a cat swishes its tail, it usually means it is unhappy about something.

Even snakes have tails. The tip of a rattlesnake's tail contains a "rattle," which makes a warning noise when the snake is about to strike.

Rattle

Tails in the Air

A bird's tail is made up of long feathers. The bird uses these feathers to help it change direction or speed.

Tail Feathers

14

Tail Feathers

15

Tails Under the Sea

Fish use their tails to help them swim. Whales use their tails to dive. A whale's tail is called a **fluke**.

Female **salmon** use their tails to dig holes in the river bottom. There they bury eggs.

17

Special Tails

Large reptiles have long tails that are very powerful. An alligator can whip its tail quickly.

19

A few **invertebrates** have tails, too. A **scorpion's** tail is rounded at the tip. It contains dangerous **venom**.

Showing Off

Some male birds use their tail feathers to attract females. The peacock spreads its beautiful tail feathers to show off for the female peahen.